GEORGE

Goes on a Plane

Nicola Smee

RGE

Goes on a Plane

ORCHARD

We're going to Spain on a PLANE to see my Uncle Teddy.

We've never flown before!

The hostess gives us some crayons and paper, and later, some drink and food in a plastic tray.

At the airport we show our tickets and passports.

Then, before we board the plane, our hand luggage is x-rayed.

X-RAY

When our seatbelts are fastened, the plane gets ready for take-off and the engines ROAR!

Look! Look, Bear! We're on top of the clouds!

Then up, up, up we go,
up into the clear blue sky.

The hostess gives us some crayons and paper, and later, some drink and food in a plastic tray.

Yum! Yum!

As we start to land,
we suck sweets to stop
our ears going 'pop'!

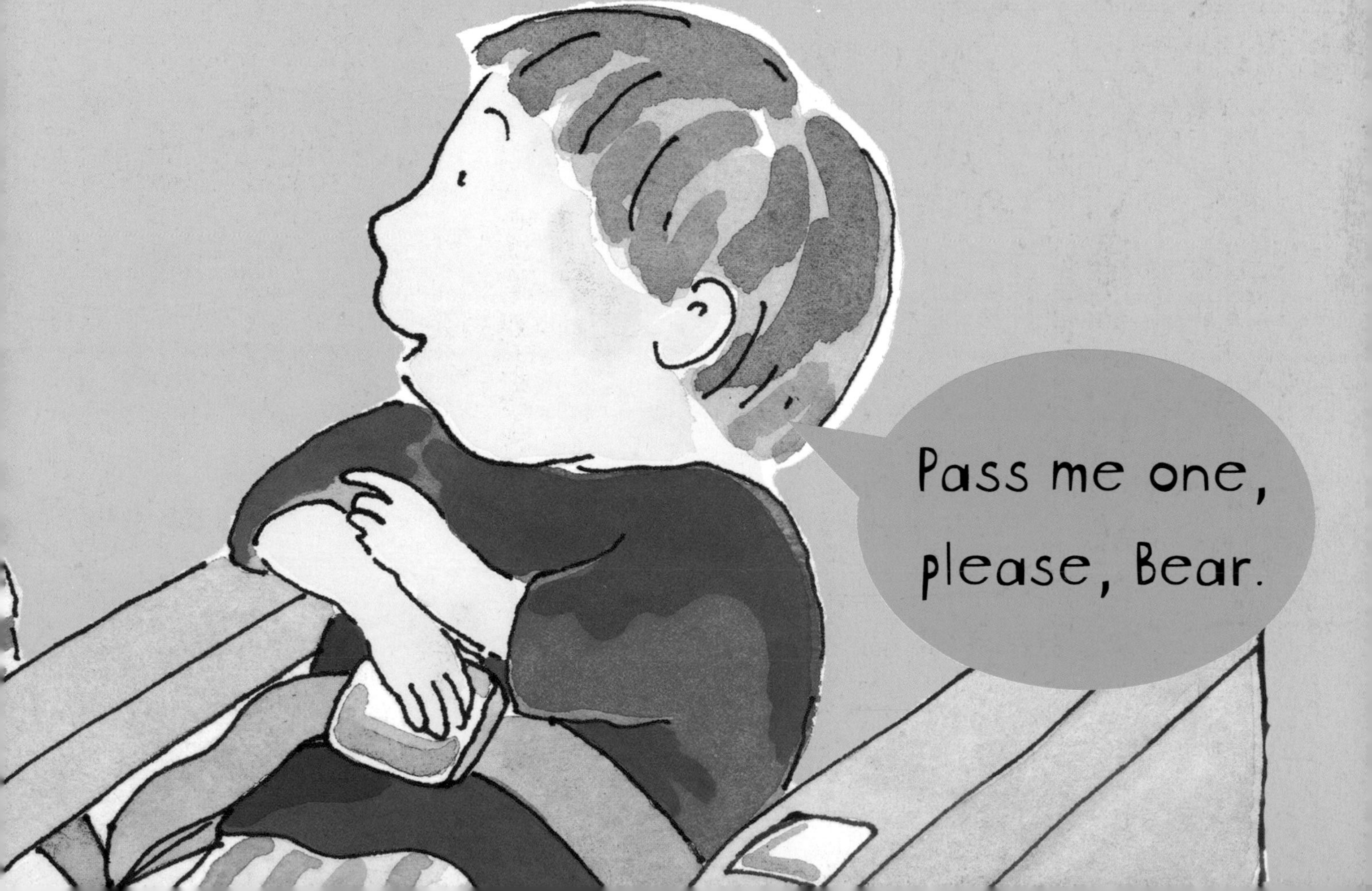

I show the hostess my pictures and she says she hopes I fly on her plane again.

Then we have to wait for our luggage to come round on the carousel.

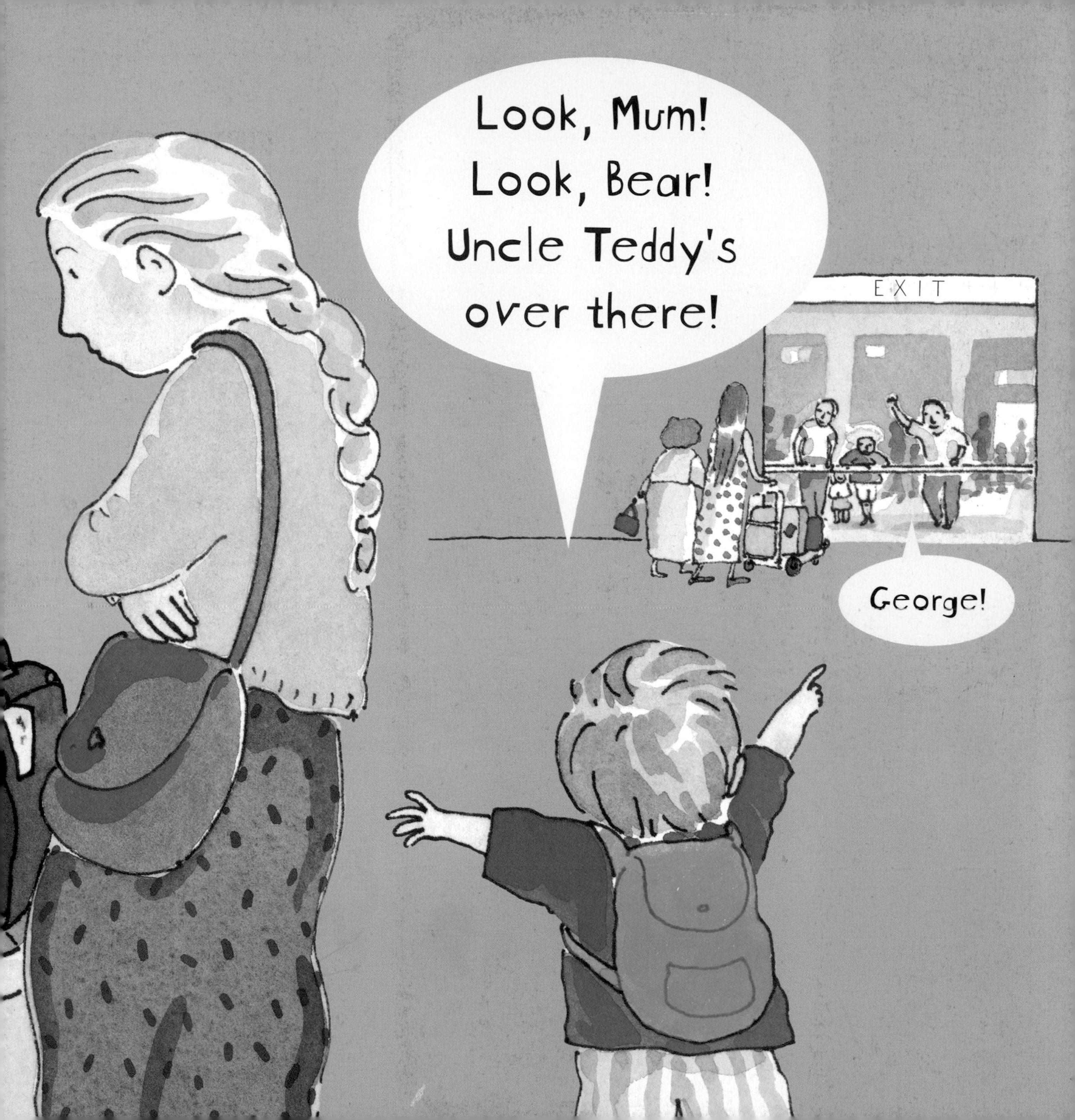
Look, Mum! Look, Bear! Uncle Teddy's over there!
EXIT
George!

ORCHARD BOOKS
338 Euston Road, London, NW1 3BH
Orchard Books Australia
Level 17/207 Kent Street, Sydney, NSW 2000
First published in 2000 by Orchard Books
This edition published 2015 • ISBN 978 1 40833 558 1
Text and illustrations © Nicola Smee 2000
The right of Nicola Smee to be identified as the author and
illustrator of this work has been asserted by her
in accordance with the Copyrights, Designs
and Patents Act, 1988.
A CIP catalogue record for this book is available from
the British Library.
1 2 3 4 5 6 7 8 9 10 • Printed in China
Orchard Books is a division of Hachette Children's Books,
an Hachette UK company.
www.hachette.co.uk